Lighten Up!

There's enough pain, suffering and stress to go around. Jesus said that while we are in this world we shall have tribulation, not may have. Though this is not very encouraging, it is necessary that we know what we're up against. The Lord is not trying to discourage us in our journey but prepare us for the road ahead. Because of His great love for us, He desires to impart everything necessary to have a joy filled life in Him.

This being the foundation of the warning sign of coming tribulation, we can now move to the next sign that reads, Lighten up! Well not really, it actually reads, be of good cheer I have overcome the world. If that promise doesn't ooze, "I got this," then nothing does. Jesus is so amazing and limitless. He tells us trouble is imminent and in the same breath proclaims we will not be overtaken as long as we look to Him.

The passion to write and illustrate a comic strip is found in this truth, that Jesus knows the world is going to be ugly and mean, yet if we gaze in His direction He has an abundance of joy, peace, happiness and yes, laughter to experience. His supply is without end, and it is His desire that we are filled with His joy and peace.

Make sure you take time to laugh today, even if you laugh at yourself, which I do quite often. Be careful you're not consumed by the weight of everyday life and spend some quality time with Christ. We know the Lord has a sense of humor; He made us.

Enjoy this collection of Preacher's Kids comic strips that span over 14 years. Hopefully they will bring a smile, perhaps stir a memory of being in a similarly humorous situation or most importantly cause you to think about the wonderful Savior who gave everything, so we could live and have life eternal.

Remember Jesus said if we refuse to become as a little child we cannot enter His kingdom, and what child is not filled with contagious laughter?

May God bless you and grant you a life filled with all the greatness He has to offer,

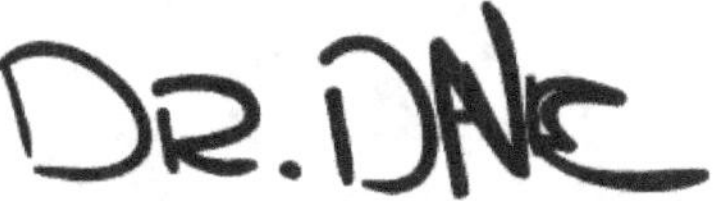

Blessed are ye
that hunger now:
for ye shall be filled.
Blessed are ye
that weep now:
for ye shall laugh.

-Luke 6:21

TODAY WE'RE GOING TO START A NEW STUDY ON THE 10 COMMANDMENTS THAT GOD GAVE TO MOSES.
I CAN ONLY COUNT UP TO 7 SO LETS JUST STUDY THE BEST ONES.
DR. DAVE

HEY PASTOR, WHAT VERSION OF THE BIBLE DO YOU PREACH OUT OF?
WELL, THIS IS A DUCT TAPE VERSION. I HAVE A GORILLA TAPE VERSION AND A SUPER GLUE VERSION AT HOME.
DR. DAVE

AARON, YOU BETTER HAVE YOUR HOMEWORK DONE BY THE TIME I COME IN THERE OR YOU ARE GOING TO BE IN BIG TROUBLE!
© 2013 DAVID AYERS WWW.PKCOMICS.COM

WELL, THAT IS GONNA DEPEND ON WHEN YOU COME IN HERE...
I THINK THINGS WOULD GO A LOT BETTER IF YOU WAITED A COUPLE OF HOURS TO COME IN.
DR. DAVE

WELL, HOW WAS CHILDREN'S CHURCH TODAY? DID YOU LEARN ANYTHING NEW?
Children's Chu
IT WAS GREAT AND YES I DID. I LEARNED THEY HAD CUPCAKES LEFT OVER FROM A SHOWER ON SATURDAY. CHILDREN'S CHURCH IS AWESOME!
DR. DAVE

AARON, WE TALKED ABOUT THE LORD'S PRAYER IN SUNDAY SCHOOL TODAY. HOW DO YOU LEARN HOW TO PRAY?
WELL... YOU LEARN TO RIDE A BIKE BY RIDING SO I GUESS YOU LEARN HOW TO PRAY BY PRAYING!
DR. DAVE

WHEN I WAS YOUR AGE I REMEMBER PLAYING IN SOME OF THE BIGGEST SNOWS.

ONE YEAR IT SNOWED SO HARD IT WAS UP TO MY WAIST... IT JUST DOESN'T SEEM TO SNOW LIKE THAT ANY MORE.

WOW DAD THAT SOUNDS LIKE A LOT OF FUN... I WISH I COULD HAVE SEEN IT.
DR. DAVE

OK WHO CAN TELL ME WHERE THE AMALEKITES WERE LOCATED?
I THINK THEY WERE BETWEEN THE FISH BITES AND THE MOSQUITO BITES.
DR. DAVE

HEY DAD, I THINK YOUR A BETTER PREACHER THAN PAUL. IN THE BIBLE IT TOOK HIM 3 HOURS TO PUT A MAN TO SLEEP AND I'VE SEEN YOU DO IT IN 30 MINUTES.
DR. DAVE

I KNOW THE BIBLE TELLS US TO LOVE OUR NEIGHBORS BUT WHAT DO WE DO IF HE PLAYS FOR THE OTHER TEAM?
HI AARON!
DR. DAVE

HEY DAD, YOU WON A VOTE WE HAD IN OUR SUNDAY SCHOOL CLASS FOR THE MOST IMPORTANT PERSON IN THE CHURCH!
GEE SON, THANKS, THAT'S QUITE AN HONOR.
© 2012 DAVID AYERS WWW.PKCOMICS.COM

YEA BUT YOU JUST WON BY ONE VOTE. THE LADIES IN THE KITCHEN MAKE A MEAN CHOCOLATE CHIP COOKIE.
Dr.Dane

COME ON DAD... PLEASE BUY US ONE!
YEA, PLEASE. 1 TIMOTHY 5:8 SAYS THAT IF YOU DON'T PROVIDE FOR YOUR FAMILY YOUR NOT BEING FAITHFUL.
TRUE... BUT I DON'T THINK BUYING YOU BOYS A JUMBO CHOCOLATE CHUNK COOKIE FALLS UNDER A PROVISION.

LORD, I KNOW YOU KNOW EVERYTHING WE DO SO I'M SURE YOU SEE THE TIMES I ONLY PRETEND TO BRUSH MY TEETH... WELL, I'M SORRY... AND YOU DON'T HAVE TO TELL MOM IF YOU DON'T WANT TO.
DR.DANE

IF THE BIBLE SAYS THE DEVIL IS A ROARING LION THEN HOW CAN WE EVER BEAT A LION?
THE ONLY WAY TO BEAT A LION IS TO CALL ON A BIGGER LION, JESUS, THE LION OF THE TRIBE OF JUDAH!
DR. DAVE

PASTOR, YOU SAID THIS MORNING WE NEED TO FOLLOW JESUS... BUT I'M HAVING TROUBLE FINDING HIS TWITTER ACCOUNT.
DR. DAVE

DING! DING! DING!
IT'S THE CHURCH BELL HONEY.
DAD WHAT IS THAT SOUND?
© 2014 DAVID AYERS WWW.PKCOMICS.COM

WE'VE ALWAYS HAD A BELL... WE JUST NEVER GOT TO CHURCH EARLY ENOUGH TO HEAR IT.
WHEN DID THE CHURCH GET A BELL?
DR. DAVE

KNOWLEDGE IS THE ABILITY TO TAKE THINGS APART AND WISDOM IS THE ABILITY TO PUT THINGS TOGETHER.
IF THAT'S TRUE, I THINK JOHN DAVID HAS MORE KNOWLEDGE THAN WISDOM.
GOD IS LOVE
DR. DAVE

I CAN'T BELIEVE YOU BEAT ME! YOU EVEN GRANNY ROLLED EVERY SHOT!
YOU MUST HAVE FORGOTTEN ABOUT DAVID AND GOLIATH... LITTLE GUYS CAN DO BIG THINGS.
DR. DAVE

YOU KNOW, BEING A KID IN KINDERGARTEN IS CONFUSING. ALL THOSE NUMBERS AND LETTERS WE HAVE TO LEARN. AND THEY EVEN EXPECT US TO STAY AWAKE AFTER LUNCH! I ALWAYS NAP AFTER LUNCH!
YOU THINK YOU'RE CONFUSED? JUST WAIT TIL YOU'RE MY AGE AND GIRLS START SMILING AND GIGGLING AT YOU. I DON'T KNOW IF I SHOULD SMILE BACK OR THROW THEM A FOOTBALL.
DR. DAVE

I JUST HEARD WE'RE TAKING YOUR FAMILY OUT FOR DINNER AFTER CHURCH TODAY.
YEA, DAD SAID SINCE YOUR DAD WAS A BAD TITHER WE NEED TO GET ALL WE CAN OUT OF HIM.
DR. DAVE

I JUST GOT A MESSAGE ON MY TABLET, WHAT DOES IDK MEAN?
I DON'T KNOW.

DAD, I GOT A MESSAGE ON MY TABLET, WHAT DOES IDK MEAN?
I DON'T KNOW.
© 2013 DAVID AYERS WWW.PKCOMICS.COM
DR. DAVE

I CAN'T BELIEVE NO ONE IN THIS HOUSE KNOWS WHAT IDK MEANS!

DID YOU SEE THAT NEW TV SHOW ABOUT THE BIBLE? IT'S GREAT! I HEARD THEY'RE EVEN COMING OUT WITH A BOOK ABOUT IT.
I THOUGHT WE ALREADY HAD A BOOK ABOUT IT... CALLED THE BIBLE.
DR. DAVE

HOW ARE YOU GOING TO GET ANY PRESENTS? YOU'VE BEEN NAUGHTY THIS YEAR!
NO I HAVEN'T, I'VE JUST BEEN A LITTLE CRANKY... BUT I'M NOT GOING TO TELL SANTA UNTIL I GET MY PRESENTS.
Santa
Santa
Dr. DAVE

HOW MANY TIMES HAVE WE TALKED ABOUT NOT DRAWING ON THE WALLS!?
NO DAD IT WASN'T ME!

REALLY... WELL I WONDER WHAT IT'S SUPPOSE TO BE?
OH, IT'S A CAT!
© 2012 DAVID AYERS WWW.PKCOMICS.COM

HEY DAD, IN 2 CORINTHIANS 13:12 THE BIBLE SAYS TO GREET ONE ANOTHER WITH A HOLY KISS... IS THAT A MISPRINT? SHOULDN'T IT SAY GREET ONE ANOTHER WITH A HERSHEY KISS?
Dr. DAVE

All the days of the afflicted are evil: but he that is of a merry heart hath a continual feast.
-Proverbs 15:15

IF JONAH RAN FROM GOD WHY DID HE STILL USE HIM TO PREACH TO THE PEOPLE OF NINEVEH?
I GUESS BECAUSE HE'S A GOD OF SECOND CHANCES.
AND THIRD AND FORTH AND FIFTH...
DR.DAVE

I HAVE TO SIT DOWN A MINUTE. I'VE BEEN KICKED IN THE SHIN, JUICE THROWN IN MY FACE, WRAPPED UP IN TOILET PAPER AND PELTED BY 50 WATER BALLOONS.
WOW, WHO DID YOU MAKE MAD AT CHURCH?
© 2012 DAVID AYERS WWW.PKCOMICS.COM

NO ONE... WE'RE JUST IN THE MIDDLE OF VACATION BIBLE SCHOOL.
DR.DAVE

DOES ANYONE KNOW WHAT NOAH BUILT?
YEA, HE BUILT A GREAT BIG BOAT!
DR.DAVE
© 2014 DAVID AYERS WWW.PKCOMICS.COM

WHO KNOWS WHAT HE PUT ON THE BOAT?
I KNOW, FISHING POLES!

WHAT ARE YOU DOING DAD?
WORKING ON OUR TAXES, THE DEADLINE IS THIS WEEK.
RENDER TO CAESAR THE THINGS THAT ARE CAESAR'S, AND TO GOD THE THINGS THAT ARE GOD'S, AND IF THERE IS ANY LEFT OVER JD AND I FOUND A NEW GAME CONSOLE WE WANT YOU TO BUY.
DR. DAVE

DO ANY OF YOU KNOW WHY NOAH BUILT THE ARK?
CAUSE HE DIDN'T WANT TO GO TO NINEVEH YOU SILLY!
DR. DAVE

SO WHAT DO YOU ALL THINK IT MUST HAVE BEEN LIKE TO LIVE IN THE GARDEN OF EDEN?
I BET IT WAS PRETTY BORING... WITH JUST 2 OF THEM THERE THEY DIDN'T HAVE ANYONE ELSE TO TALK ABOUT.
DR. DAVE

THIS STINKS...
I'M IN SKITS FOR VBS THIS YEAR AND OUR THEME IS OUTER SPACE,
SO I HAVE TO BE PLUTO AND IT'S NOT EVEN A REAL PLANET!
DR. DAVE

AARON THOMAS AYERS! GET IN HERE!
SOMETIMES I THINK THE ONLY REASON I HAVE A MIDDLE NAME IS TO KNOW WHEN I'M IN TROUBLE.
DR. DAVE

WHAT DO YOU MEAN OUR BIBLE DRILL CLASS IS CANCELLED?!
WHAT GOOD IS HAVING ALL THESE VERSES I MEMORIZED FLOATING AROUND IN MY HEAD IF I CAN'T SHARE THEM WITH SOMEONE?!
DR. DAVE

WELL BOYS, SPRING CAMP FOR THE CHURCH YOUTH IS COMING UP IN A COUPLE OF WEEKS, ARE YOU ALL READY?
I DON'T MIND CAMPING IF THERE'S PLENTY OF DRINKS, JUNK FOOD AND WIFI. OH AND I WOULD RATHER CAMP INSIDE INSTEAD OF OUTSIDE.
DR. DAVE

MOO!
BAHHH!
I FORGOT HOW A DONKEY SOUNDS!
Dr. DAVE

SNOW IS A LOT LIKE JESUS. JESUS COVERS A MULTITUDE OF SIN AND SNOW COVERS A MULTITUDE OF YARD WORK.
DR. DAVE

WOULD YOU LIKE SALAD OR SLAW WITH THAT?
I THINK I WILL HAVE SLAW.

WHY DID YOU ORDER SLAW? YOU DON'T EVEN LIKE IT!
I KNOW, I WAS AFRAID IF I ORDERED SOMETHING I LIKE I WOULD EAT IT AND GET TOO FULL AND SPOIL MY SUPPER.

DAD... HOW COME PEOPLE AT CHURCH ARE ALWAYS ASKING YOU HOW YOU ARE DOING BUT YOU NEVER ASK ANYONE HOW THEY ARE DOING?
BECAUSE, I'M AFRAID THEY WILL TELL ME.

JOHN DAVID.

JOHN DAVID!

JOHN DAVID!!!
COMING!

CAN'T RESPOND TOO QUICK OR HE WILL START TO EXPECT IT ALL THE TIME.

MOM SAID WE CAN'T HAVE COOKIES UNTIL AFTER SUPPER... WOULD IT BE WRONG TO GO OVER HER HEAD AND ASK GOD?
COOKIE
DR. DAVE

WITH ALL THESE COLORS WHY ARE YOU JUST COLORING BLUE EGGS?
WELL... LAST YEAR ALL I COULD FIND WERE BLUE EGGS, SO THIS YEAR I'M JUST MAKING SURE THERE ARE PLENTY OF THEM.
DR. DAVE

THE SPIRIT IS WILLING
JUST ORDER YOGURT, JUST ORDER YOGURT.
© 2012 DAVID AYERS WWW.PKCOMICS.COM

BUT THE FLESH IS WEAK
I'LL HAVE THREE SCOOPS OF THE DOUBLE CHOCOLATE FUDGE ICE CREAM ON A WAFFLE CONE, PLEASE.
DR. DAVE

GALATIANS 5:14 STATES, "FOR THE LAW IS FULFILLED IN ONE WORD, EVEN IN THIS, THOU SHALT LOVE THY NEIGHBOR AS THYSELF." WHAT DO YOU GUYS THINK ABOUT THAT VERSE?
I THINK THAT'S MORE THAN ONE WORD.
DR. DAVE

DAD, I'M TEACHING SUNDAY SCHOOL THIS WEEKEND FOR YOUTH SUNDAY. CAN YOU GIVE ME YOUR NOTES ON ONE OF YOUR GOOD SERMONS WHEN PEOPLE DIDN'T FALL ASLEEP?
#1 DAD
DR. DAVE

I LOVE THANKSGIVING LEFTOVERS BUT WHEN YOU EAT LIKE MY FAMILY THERE ISN'T MUCH FOOD LEFTOVER.
CHIPS
DR. DAVE

HEY JOHN DAVID, HE'S GOT YOUR TOY. ARE YOU NOT GOING TO GET IT BACK?
SEE, THAT'S THE PROBLEM WITH THE WORLD TODAY... ALL THE PEOPLE THAT NEED STANDING UP TO ARE ENORMOUS.
YS
DR. DAVE

SORRY DAD, I FORGOT AND RODE THE BUS AGAIN. GOOD THING THE BUS DRIVER HAS A CELL PHONE OR I WOULDN'T KNOW WHAT TO DO.

THANKS... I FIGURE IF I DO THIS ENOUGH I'LL GET MY OWN CELL PHONE.
DR. DAVE

HERE JD, HERE'S A BROWNIE FOR YOU AND ONE FOR ME.
THAT'S NOT VERY NICE. YOU GAVE ME THE SMALLER PIECE. IF I WERE HANDING THEM OUT I WOULD GIVE YOU THE BIGGER PIECE!

WELL I'VE GOT THE BIGGER PIECE! WHAT ARE YOU COMPLAINING ABOUT?
DR. DAVE

Then was our mouth filled with laughter, and our tongue with singing:

-Psalm 126:2

DAD YOU KNOW HOW PEOPLE ARE ALWAYS ASKING SINGERS TO SING ONE MORE SONG? WELL, WHY DON'T PEOPLE ASK YOU TO PREACH ONE MORE VERSE?
YOUTH CAM
SWIM FOO
HIKE
RAFTI
DR. DAVE

AARON WILL YOU LEAD US IN PRAYER TO START OUR YOUTH RETREAT?
THANK YOU GOD FOR LETTING US GO ON THIS RETREAT... HELP US NOT DO ANYTHING STUPID... AMEN.
© 2013 DAVID AYERS WWW.PKCOMICS.COM

I COULDN'T HAVE SAID IT BETTER MYSELF.
DR. DAVE

PASTOR, I DON'T MEAN TO SOUND LIKE I'M FULL OF SELF PITY BUT... WHY DOES EVERYTHING BAD IN THE ENTIRE WORLD ALWAYS HAPPEN TO ME?
DR. DAVE

TURN IN YOUR BIBLES TO MATTHEW CHAPTER 18.
Dr. Dave

WELL... IT'S NAP TIME, WAKE ME UP WHEN DAD IS FINISHED.
© 2014 DAVID AYERS WWW.PKCOMICS.COM

I WANT THE COOLEST TOY IN THE WHOLE WORLD... HOW MUCH IS IT BECAUSE I ONLY HAVE TEN DOLLARS?
BOB'S TOY ZONE
NEW
DR. DAVE

DAD HURRY! WE HAVE TO GET TO 3RD STREET. JOEY JUST POSTED ON FACEBOOK THAT THE OGLES ARE GIVING AWAY CARAMEL APPLES AND THEY ONLY HAVE 6 APPLES LEFT!
YEA DAD LET'S GO!
EVEN TRICK-OR-TREAT HAS FALLEN VICTIM TO ADVANCED TECHNOLOGY.
DR. DAVE

SO NOW THAT WE HAVE READ THE 10 COMMANDMENTS, WHAT DO YOU ALL THINK ABOUT THEM?
WHOEVER "THOU" IS, GOD SURE HAS A LOT OF THINGS HE CAN'T DO... I'M GLAD THAT'S NOT ME.
DR. DAVE

ARE YOU GOING TO SLED DOWN THAT HILL JOHN DAVID? IT SURE LOOKS DANGEROUS.
SURE I AM... DANGER IS MY MIDDLE NAME, ONLY I SPELL IT D-A-V-I-D.
DR. DAVE

WELL BOYS, HOW WAS YOUR FIRST WEEK BACK AT SCHOOL?
I'M DOING ALRIGHT, MAKING GOOD GRADES, THE FUTURE'S SO BRIGHT, I GOTTA WEAR SHADES...
YOU HAVE TO STOP LISTENING TO DAD'S 80'S STATION ON HIS XM RADIO.
DR. DAVE

I LOVE THESE PLASTIC EGGS. THEY'RE GREAT TO BUST OPEN AND SEE THE TREASURE THAT'S HIDDEN INSIDE. IT CAN BE CANDY OR A TOY, DOESN'T MATTER, I LIKE IT ALL!
ME TOO... THAT'S JUST LIKE JESUS AND THE FIRST EASTER. HE WAS IN THE TOMB AND BUSTED OUT TO BE A TREASURE TO THE WHOLE WORLD.
DR. DAVE

DAD, I DON'T THINK THIS IS THE WAY TO MY FRIENDS HOUSE.
YEA, NOTHING LOOKS FAMILIAR. ARE YOU SURE YOU KNOW WHERE WE ARE?
I'M NOT EXACTLY SURE... BUT WE SEEM TO BE MAKING GOOD TIME!
DR. DAVE

B C
JOHN DAVID! WAKE UP!
Z Z Z Z Z
© 2012 DAVID AYERS WWW.PKCOMICS.COM

OH, I WASN'T ASLEEP, MY EYES WERE JUST WINKING REALLY FAST.
DR. DAVE

LORD REMEMBER PSALM 43:1, "YOU BE MY JUDGE, GOD, AND PLEAD MY CASE AGAINST AN UNHOLY NATION; RESCUE ME FROM THE DECEITFUL AND UNJUST MAN."
Office of the Principal
Dr. DAVE

I CAN'T EVEN PICK OUT A VALENTINE FOR ONE GIRL... HOW DID SOLOMON BUY FOR 700 WIVES AND NOT GET THE SAME CARD?
TELL ME ABOUT IT. GOD MAY HAVE MADE HIM THE WISEST KING BUT IN THE ROMACE DEPARTMENT HE WAS DUMB AS A ROCK.
LOVE
Dr. DAVE

DAD, I KNOW THAT YOU'RE GETTING OLDER BUT... YOU STILL LOOK PRETTY GOOD AFTER HAVING TWO KIDS!
Dr. DAVE

FOOTBALL IS THE BEST!
NO, BASEBALL IS BEST!
WELL... I THINK SOCCER IS FUN.

SIGH...

YEA, SOCCER IS FUN.
© 2013 DAVID AYERS WWW.PKCOMICS.COM
DR. DAVE

I'M STARVING AND THERE'S NOTHING IN THE HOUSE TO EAT.
IN THE WORLD YE SHALL HAVE TRIBULATION.
BUT BE OF GOOD CHEER I HAVE OVERCOME THE WORLD!
China House
China House
DR. DAVE

WELL, NOW THAT WE'RE GRADUATING KINDERGARTEN DO YOU THINK WE WILL HAVE TO GO LOOK FOR A JOB?
I DON'T KNOW... BUT WHOEVER HIRES ME, I HOPE THEY STILL LET ME HAVE A JUICE BOX BEFORE NAPTIME.
DR. DAVE

OK DAD, WE'VE GOT THE TREE DECORATED. YOU JUST NEED TO COME IN AND PUT THE STAR ON TOP!
DR. DAVE

I HATE SCHOOL. I WISH WE COULD JUST GO HOME AFTER LUNCH.
DR. DAVE

THAT NEW GIRL IN CLASS TOLD MARSHA THAT SHE THINKS YOUR CUTE.
© 2013 DAVID AYERS WWW.PKCOMICS.COM

WHAT ARE YOU WAITING FOR! LET'S HURRY BACK TO CLASS BEFORE WE'RE LATE!

HOW CAN YOU DRINK A MILKSHAKE THROUGH A STRAW AND STILL GET IT ALL OVER YOUR SHIRT?
I DON'T KNOW... I GUESS I'M JUST TALENTED THAT WAY.
DR. DAVE

DO YOU SEE HOW CRAZY THAT GUY IS DRIVING?
YEA AND HIS BUMPER STICKER SAYS, "I FOLLOW JESUS."
MAYBE HE JUST FOLLOWS HIM ON SUNDAY.
DR. DAVE

HEY 3 DAYS AGO MY PLASTIC EGGS HAD CANDY IN THEM! WHERE IS MY CANDY?!
THAT'S JUST LIKE JESUS IN THE TOMB. 3 DAYS LATER THE TOMB WAS EMPTY.
© 2012 DAVID AYERS WWW.PKCOMICS.COM
DR. DAVE

STOP TRYING TO CHANGE THE SUBJECT, THIS IS SERIOUS! SOMEONE STOLE MY CANDY!
DR. DAVE

MY ARM'S GETTING TIRED FROM WRITING ALL THESE VALENTINE CARDS FOR MY CLASS.
YOU THINK YOU'RE TIRED? IMAGINE HOW TIRED GOD GETS WRITING VALENTINE CARDS, EVERYBOY IS HIS VALENTINE!
DR. DAVE

A time to weep, and a time to laugh; a time to mourn, and a time to dance;

-Ecclesiastes 3:4

LORD, I PRAY FOR SAFETY FOR OUR CHURCH FAMILY. HELP EVERYONE LIVE IN HARMONY AND KEEP SICKNESS FAR AWAY. LET NO ONE DIE AND KEEP ANY THOUGHTS OF MARRIAGE AWAY UNTIL NEXT WEEK. AND IF YOU DON'T MIND, CAUSE THE CHURCH TO LOSE MY PHONE NUMBER FOR AT LEAST THE NEXT 3 HOURS. AMEN.
© 2015 DAVID AYERS WWW.PKCOMICS.COM

NOW LET'S GET READY FOR THE SUPER BOWL!!!!!
DR. DAVE

DAD, JD AND I WANT YOU TO HELP US SET UP A LEMONADE STAND.
WITH THE COST AND TIME THIS DOESN'T LOOK TOO GOOD.

TELL YOU WHAT, WHY DON'T I JUST GIVE YOU BOTH $5 AND WE ALL CALL IT A DAY?

SEE I TOLD YOU THE OLD, "HELP US BUILD A LEMONADE STAND" TRICK WAS GOOD FOR A FEW BUCKS.
DR. DAVE

ISN'T THE 4TH OF JULY THE GREATEST!
I'M NOT SURE... ALL I HEAR IS, DO YOUR HOMEWORK, CLEAN UP YOUR ROOM, EAT ALL YOUR VEGETABLES! IF WE'RE CELEBRATING FREEDOM THEN WHY IS EVERYONE STILL TELLING ME WHAT TO DO?!
DR. DAVE

HEY DAD, IF 15 YEAR OLD KATIE LEDECKY CAN WIN AN OLYMPIC GOLD MEDAL, IT GIVES ME HOPE THAT A LITTLE GUY LIKE ME CAN DO GREAT THINGS, SO I'M STARTING NOW TO TRAIN FOR THE OLYMPIC SWIMMING TEAM!
WITH A LITTLE FAITH YOU CAN DO MORE THAN YOU KNOW LITTLE MAN.
DR. DAVE
3

I SAW IN THE BULLETIN SUNDAY THAT WE'RE HAVING A POTLUCK DINNER NEXT WEEK AFTER WORSHIP.
I LOVE POTLUCK DINNERS. IT'S GREAT TO GET TOGETHER WITH EVERYONE.
YEA, AS LONG AS YOU EAT OUT OF THE LUCKY POT... THE UNLUCKY POTS HAVE ALL VEGETABLES IN THEM.
DR. DAVE

SO, JOHN DAVID, SINCE IT'S THANKSGIVING, WHAT ARE YOU THANKFUL FOR?
WELL... I'M THANKFUL FOR MY FAMILY, MY CHURCH, GETTING OUT OF SCHOOL AND THAT I'M STUFFED WITH TURKEY INSTEAD A STUFFED TURKEY.
DR. DAVE

I'M NOT CATCHING ANYTHING... I'M BORED...
TOO BAD WE'RE NOT FISHING WITH JESUS, I BET HE KNEW WHERE ALL THE FISH WERE BITING.
Dr. Dave

...AND THANK YOU LORD FOR SARAH JOSEPHA HALE. IF SHE HADN'T PUSHED THE PRESIDENT TO MAKE THANKSGIVING A NATIONAL HOLIDAY WE WOULDN'T GET THESE TWO AND A HALF DAYS OUT OF SCHOOL TO PIG OUT AND WATCH FOOTBALL! -AMEN!
Dr. Dave

OH, PASTOR, IF YOU'RE GOING TO LEAVE A TRACK, LEAVE ONE WITHOUT THE CHURCH NAME ON IT... I ONLY HAVE A COUPLE OF DOLLARS FOR A TIP.
Dr. Dave

I LOVE YOUR SHIRT! IT SUITS YOU PERFECTLY!
Easily Distracted

Easily Distracted
DR. DAVE
© 2013 DAVID AYERS WWW.PKCOMICS.COM

WHAT?
Easily Distracted

YOU BOYS SEEM TO NEVER WORRY ABOUT ANYTHING. I WISH I COULD BE AS CARE FREE AS YOU. HOW DO YOU DO IT?
IT'S EASY, IF SOMETHING STARTS TO WORRY ME I JUST GIVE IT TO GOD... HE'S GOING TO BE UP ALL NIGHT ANYWAY.
DR. DAVE

I CAN'T FIGURE OUT WHY ATTENDANCE HAS DROPPED OFF. I WONDER IF IT'S SOMETHING THAT I'VE DONE?
OH, I DIDN'T KNOW THE CHURCH HAD TO BE FULL TO MEAN YOU'RE A GOOD PREACHER!
© 2013 DAVID AYERS WWW.PKCOMICS.COM

"OUT OF THE MOUTH OF BABES YOU HAVE ORDAINED STRENGTH," THANK YOU LORD.
DR. DAVE

WHAT DOES IT MEAN WHEN PEOPLE SAY, "THE APPLE DOESN'T FALL FAR FROM THE TREE?"
IT MEANS WHEN WE GET OLD WE'RE GOING TO HAVE THIN HAIR, WATCH OLD BLACK AND WHITE MOVIES AND LISTEN TO BING CROSBY AT CHRISTMAS.
DR.DAVE

YOU KNOW, THESE HORNETS ARE A LOT LIKE THE DEVIL. IT SEEMS THEIR ONLY JOB IS TO STING US AND MAKE US FEEL MISERABLE.
YOU'RE RIGHT. THAT'S WHY I'M GLAD JESUS IS LIKE A NEW CAN OF HORNET SPRAY!
HORNET WASP
DR.DAVE

WOW, I CAN'T BELIEVE IT'S ALREADY 2015! THIS YEAR HAS GONE BY FAST. TIME FLIES WHEN YOU'RE OLDER, RIGHT DAD?
WHAT ARE YOU SAYING? DO YOU GUYS REALLY THINK I LOOK A LOT OLDER?
NO DAD, YOU DON'T LOOK TOO OLD. YOU'RE JUST LIKE YOUR SHIRT, A LITTLE WRINKLED.
DR.DAVE

GOD I HAVE A TEST COMING UP, IF YOU HELP ME AND MY TEACHER FINDS OUT WILL THAT BE CONSIDERED CHEATING?
DR. DAVE

I BET DAD IS BUMMED OUT HAVING TO STAY HOME ON SPRING BREAK WITH LARYNGITIS AND IT'S JUST A FEW DAYS TIL SUNDAY. HOW WILL HE PREACH?
I KNOW... HOW WILL PEOPLE KNOW HOW SMART HE IS IF HE CAN'T TALK?
DR. DAVE

NEXT ITEM, WHAT SHOULD OUR CLUB BE CALLED?
LET'S CALL IT THE WARRIORS!
NO, HOW BOUT THE AVENGERS?
I LIKE THE BATCAVE!
WE SOUND AS BAD AS SOME OF DAD'S BUSINESS MEETINGS AT CHURCH.
DR. DAVE

OK PREACHER, I'M READY TO BE BAPTIZED AND I BROUGHT MY STUFF TO GO SWIMMING AFTERWARD!
Dr. Dave

HEY DAD, CAN I GO TO JOEY'S HOUSE AGAIN TOMORROW?
NO SON... YOU WERE THERE FOR 4 HOURS TODAY.
© 2012 DAVID AYERS WWW.PKCOMICS.COM

BUT IT'S OK, JOEY'S MOM SAID I COULD COME OVER ANYTIME, SHE SAID I HAD A STANDING OVATION.
Dr. Dave

HEY! WHO ATE MY LAST DONUT?! IT WAS THE CHOCOLATE ONE!
HOW SHOULD WE KNOW IT WAS YOURS? IT DIDN'T HAVE YOUR NAME ON IT.
DONUTS
© 2014 DAVID AYERS WWW.PKCOMICS.COM

IT HAD SPRINKLES ON IT... IT MIGHT AS WELL HAVE HAD MY NAME ON IT!
Dr. Dave

© 2015 DAVID AYERS WWW.PKCOMICS.COM

A merry heart doeth good like a medicine: but a broken spirit drieth the bones.

-Proverbs 17:22

MY SHOULDERS ARE SUNBURNED, SALT WATER IN MY EYES AND SAND IN MY SHORTS... MANY ARE THE AFFLICTIONS OF THE RIGHTEOUS...
BUT THE LORD DELIVERETH HIM OUT OF THEM ALL!
DR. DAVE

WHO WAS IT THAT KILLED THE GIANT?
IT WAS JACK.
I THOUGHT IT WAS DAVID.
DR. DAVE

I GUESS IT DEPENDS ON WHAT BOOK YOU READ.
© 2013 DAVID AYERS WWW.PKCOMICS.COM

SO HOW IS THAT HISTORY CLASS GOING THIS YEAR?
NO WORRIES DAD THAT CLASS IS GOING TO BE AN EASY A.
© 2012 DAVID AYERS WWW.PKCOMICS.COM

OH GREAT! SO WHAT DO YOU HAVE IN IT SO FAR?
B-

YOU KNOW, THE BIBLE SAYS WE WOULD HAVE DAYS LIKE THIS.
55
31
DR.DAVE
FOOTBALL TRY OUTS

I DON'T LIKE OUR NEIGHBORS.
DIDN'T JESUS SAY WE SHOULD LOVE OUR NEIGHBORS?
YEA BUT I BET JESUS DIDN'T LIVE NEXT TO A GUY WITH A SIGN THAT SAYS, "KEEP OUT, DOG BITES AND OWNER SHOOTS."
KEEP OUT
KEEP OUT
DR.DAVE

SO DAD, DO YOU LIKE THE PRESENT WE GOT YOU FOR FATHER'S DAY?
I GUESS... BUT ISN'T THIS OUR TV REMOTE?
YEA BUT FOR TODAY WE'RE GOING TO ACTUALLY LET YOU USE IT!
DR.DAVE

YOU KNOW... I'VE ALWAYS WONDERED IF A PUMPKIN WAS A FRUIT OR A VEGETABLE.
YUCK! YOU MEAN PEOPLE REALLY EAT THESE THINGS? I JUST THOUGHT THEY WERE FOR DECORATION.
DR. DAVE

DAD, IS IT OK FOR ME TO TALK ABOUT SOMEONE AS LONG AS I SAY, "BLESS THEIR HEART" AFTER I'M DONE?
DR. DAVE

YOU'RE A PRETTY COOL DAD, I HOPE I CAN GROW UP TO BE BIG AND STRONG LIKE YOU ONE DAY!

YOU'RE A PRETY COOL DAD, I HOPE I CAN GROW UP TO BE BIG AND STRONG LIKE YOU ONE DAY!
DR. DAVE

41

AARON, HOW IS YOUR SUMMER JOB MOWING YARDS GOING?
PRETTY GOOD... I'M ALMOST MAKING AS MUCH AS I'M SPENDING!
Dr. DAVE

HOW WAS FOOTBALL PRACTICE?
I FUMBLED SEVEN TIMES, GOT SOME CUTS, SCRAPES, BRUISES AND HAD TO BE CARRIED OFF THE FIELD. THEN I GOT DIZZY AND HAD TO GET A DRINK OF WATER AND LATER THREW UP... BUT BESIDES THAT I THINK I DID PRETTY GOOD.
DR. DAVE

HAPPY FATHER'S DAY TO THE SECOND BEST DAD IN THE WORLD... WELL, YOU KNOW, GOD GETS TOP BILLING AS THE BEST FATHER BUT YOU'RE SECOND!
NO WORRIES BOYS, I'LL BE HONORED TO COME SECOND TO GOD IN ANYTHING, AND ESPECIALLY FATHERHOOD.
DR. DAVE

GATHER ROUND BOYS, THE PASTOR IS GOING TO LEAD US IN PRAYER BEFORE THE KICKOFF!
PASTOR, THE LAST TIME YOU PRAYED BEFORE OUR GAME, I GOT A BLOODY NOSE, JOEY GOT A SPRAINED ANKLE AND BOBBY LOST A TOOTH... WOULD IT BE OK IF YOU WAITED AND PRAYED FOR US AFTER THE GAME?
DR. DAVE

THIS CATALOG HAS TOO MANY HALLOWEEN COSTUMES IN IT! I CAN'T DECIDE. I WISH THE RIGHT ONE WAS EASY TO PICK AND I DIDN'T HAVE TO CHOOSE.
THAT WOULD BE AWESOME! JUST THINK IF WE ALWAYS CHOSE THE RIGHT THING... WE WOULD ALWAYS PLEASE GOD AND HAVE THE COOLEST COSTUMES FOR HALLOWEEN!
DR. DAVE

I WONDER WHY PEOPLE ARE ALWAYS SAYING YOU LOOK LIKE ME?
I KNOW WHY. MY WHOLE LIFE ALL I'VE EVER WORN IS YOUR HAND-ME-DOWNS. OF COURSE THEY THINK I LOOK LIKE YOU!
DR. DAVE

HEY DAD WHAT IS EARTH DAY?
I'M NOT SURE. I GUESS A DAY WE SHOULD CELEBRATE THE EARTH.
WHY CELEBRATE THE EARTH WHEN WE CAN CELEBRATE THE ONE WHO MADE THE EARTH?
DR. DAVE

HEY PASTOR, HAVE YOU TRIED THE CHOCOLATE PIE? IT"S DELICIOUS!
GET THEE BEHIND ME SATAN!!!!
I'LL HAVE TO APPOLOGIZE FOR DAD, THIS NEW DIET HE'S ON DOESN'T INCLUDE CHOCOLATE AND HE'S A LITTLE BIT ON EDGE.
DR. DAVE

DEAR JESUS, HELP ME TO BE MORE LIKE YOU AND LESS LIKE ME. AMEN.
DR. DAVE

IT'S STILL RAINING! I WISH THE SUN WOULD COME OUT!
WE LEARNED IN SCHOOL THE SUN DOESN'T GO AWAY IN A STORM, IT'S STILL UP THERE SHINING EVEN THOUGH THE CLOUDS TRY TO HIDE IT FROM US.
HOW TRUE, THE SON IS ALWAYS SHINING EVEN THOUGH SOMETIMES WE CAN'T SEE.
DR. DAVE

WELL, WE'RE GONNA MISS OUR PET BIRD COCOA... WOULD YOU GUYS LIKE TO SAY SOMETHING?
I THINK WE OUGHT TO SING A SONG... BUT WHICH ONE?
I'LL FLY AWAY... DUH!
COCOA
DR. DAVE

DAD! YOU'RE GOING TO HAVE TO HELP ME. I CAN'T FIND ANY EGGS. YOU HID THEM TOO GOOD.
I COULD ONLY HIDE SO MANY BETWEEN THE COUCH AND TV. YOU MAY HAVE TO LOOK A LITTLE HARDER.
DR. DAVE

YOU MAY THINK YOU ARE ONLY SNOW, ROCKS & CARROTS BUT JUST AS GOD SAID TO GIDEON, "I SEE MIGHTY SNOWMEN OF VALOR!"
DR. DAVE

DO YOU HAVE YOUR LINES MEMORIZED FOR THE CHRISTMAS PLAY?
I BRING YOU GOOD TIDINGS OF GREAT JOY WHICH SHALL BE TO ALL PEOPLE. FOR UNTO YOU IS BORN THIS DAY IN THE CITY OF DAVID A SAVIOR WHICH IS CHRIST THE LORD... I'M RECITING FROM THE GOSPEL OF LUKE.
I THOUGHT LINUS WAS THE ONE WHO SAID THAT.. WHO IS LUKE? WAS HE IN A CHARLIE BROWN CHRISTMAS?
DR. DAVE

SPRING BREAK IS ALMOST OVER THEN IT'S BACK TO SCHOOL.
I'M JUST IN KINDERGARTEN AND I ALREADY HATE HAVING TO STUDY.
BETTER HOPE GOD DOESN'T CALL YOU TO PREACH. DAD SAYS HE STUDIES MORE NOW THAN HE EVER DID IN SCHOOL.
DR. DAVE

PASTOR, YOU KNOW HOW YOU CAN TRADE PLAYERS YOU DON'T WANT ON A FANTASY FOOTBALL LEAGUE, WELL, WHAT IF THERE WAS A FANTASY CHURCH LEAGUE AND YOU COULD TRADE MEMBERS THAT YOU DIDN'T WANT TO OTHER CHURCHES?
© 2014 DAVID AYERS WWW.PKCOMICS.COM

PASTOR?! I WAS JUST KIDDING...
DR. DAVE

WE NEED TO SAY A PRAYER FOR YOUR COUSIN. HE GOES IN THIS WEEK TO GET HIS WISDOM TEETH TAKEN OUT.
IF THEY'RE CALLED WISDOM TEETH THEN WHY DO WE TAKE THEM OUT! THE BIBLE TELLS US TO PRAY FOR WISDOM... NO WONDER WE'RE LIVING IN A WORLD FULL OF GOOFBALLS!
DR. DAVE

DID YOU KNOW THE SQUARE ROOT OF 26 IS 5.0990195135927845?
NO BUT TODAY WE LEARNED THAT THIS IS AN S.
S
SNAKE
DR. DAVE

WHY ARE YOU STILL MAD? JOSEPH FORGAVE HIS BROTHERS AFTER THEY TRIED TO KILL HIM. I DIDN'T DO ANYTHING NEAR THAT BAD.
MAYBE NOT BUT TAKING A BITE OF MY PEANUT BUTTER AND JELLY SANDWICH IS A PRETTY SERIOUS OFFENCE.
DR. DAVE

AARON, READ ME THE BIBLE STORY ABOUT THE BIG FISH.
THE STORY OF JONAH AND THE WHALE?

NO, THE ONE ABOUT PETER CATCHING A FISH WITH A COIN IN ITS MOUTH. OUR SCOUT TROOP IS GOING FISHING TOMORROW AND I WANT TO KNOW WHAT KIND OF BAIT HE USED.
DR. DAVE
© 2012 DAVID AYERS WWW.PKCOMICS.COM

DAD, I ALWAYS HATE IT WHEN YOU OR MOM CALL ME BY MY FULL NAME, I KNOW I'M IN TROUBLE.
JUST WAIT UNTIL YOU GET MARRIED AND YOUR WIFE CALLS YOU BY YOUR FULL NAME... NOW THAT'S BIG TROUBLE.
TIMES
DR. DAVE

HEY DAD, FOR NO REASON AT ALL I JUST WANT YOU TO KNOW HOW MUCH I LOVE YOU AND APPRECIATE YOU... AND WHILE WE'RE HERE TALKING, DO YOU THINK I COULD HAVE TWENTY DOLLARS?
DR. DAVE

NOW THAT YOU'RE WORKING THIS SUMMER AARON YOU CAN SPEND SOME OF YOUR MONEY BUT YOU NEED TO SAVE MOST OF IT FOR THE FUTURE.
DR. DAVE
BUT DAD I WANTED TO BUY A FEW MORE VIDEO GAMES AND SOME COMIC BOOKS!
WHY IS IT PARENTS ARE ALWAYS WORRIED ABOUT OUR FUTURE AND NOBODY IS WORRIED ABOUT OUR RIGHT NOW?!

SO WHAT DO YOU THINK OF THAT NEW KID JAKE IN OUR CLASS? I LIKE HIM, HE'S FUNNY.
WE DON'T HAVE A JAKE IN OUR CLASS.
DR. DAVE

I KNOW... HE JUST LOOKS LIKE A JAKE SO THAT'S WHAT I CALL HIM.